To my siblings and step-siblings: Felicity, David, Gréagóir, Jim, Marian, Raphael, Micheál, Denis, Cathy and Doug
— M. D.

To Therese, who understands a child's sense of wonder
— W. H.

This text is based on traditional rhymes and incantations that have been passed down from child to child for generations — in skipping games, ball bouncing and counting people out. Many of these rhymes are Irish and bring back fond memories of my childhood in Whitehead, County Antrim.

— M. D.

One, two, three O'Leary,
Four, five, six O'Leary,
Seven, eight, nine O'Leary,
Ten O'Leary children.

Ibble obble,
Blue bottle,
Ibble obble out.
Turn your silk pyjamas
Inside out.

First you turn them inside,
Then you turn them out.
Ibble obble,
Blue bottle,
Ibble obble OUT!

Red, white and blue,
The cat's got flu,
The dog's got chicken pox,
And OUT goes you!

Ingle, angle,
Silver bangle,
Put your washing through the mangle.
Ingle, angle,
Silver bangle,
Ingle, angle, OUT!

Eeny, meeny, macka racka,
Em, oh, dominacka,
Alla backa, sugaracka,
Om, pom, PUSH!

One, two, three,
Mother caught a flea.
She put it in the teapot
And made a cup of tea.

The flea jumped out.
Mother gave a shout,
And in came Father
With his shirt hanging OUT!

Hickety pickety, eye silickity,
Pompalorum jig.
I wish I hadn't any hair
So I could wear a wig.
One, two, three,
OUT goes he!

What's your name?
Mary Jane.
Where do you live?
Down the lane.
What do you have?
I've a shop.

What do you sell?
Ginger pop.
How many bottles
In a day?
Twenty-four,
Now GO AWAY!

Icker backer,
Soda cracker,
Icker backer boo.
Number two O'Leary —
OUT goes you!

One O'Leary in the bed,
Dozing like a sleepyhead.
In came the bogeyman . . .

. . . and OUT went she.

"Hey," said Mrs O'Leary, "that's not fair."
"Maybe," said the bogeyman,
"but I don't care!"

Jelly on a plate, jelly on a plate,
Wibble wobble, wibble wobble,
Jelly on a plate.

Sausage in the pan, sausage in the pan,
Turn it over, turn it over,
Sausage in the pan.

Apple in a tree, apple in a tree,
Shaker shaker, shaker shaker,
Apple in a tree.
Bogey in the bed, bogey in the bed,
Kick him OUT and kick him OUT,
The bogey in the bed.

Who shaved the bogeyman,
The bogeyman, the bogeyman?
Who shaved the bogeyman?
The bogey shaved himself.

Who put on his waistcoat,
His waistcoat, his waistcoat?
Who put on his waistcoat?
He put it on himself.

Catch him by the waistcoat,
The jacket and the overcoat.
Tell him he's a billy goat
And CHASE HIM DOWN THE STAIRS!

"Open the door and let us in, sir.
We are frozen to the skin, sir.
Open the door and let us in, sir,
Early in the morning."

"Okay, in you come!"

One, two, three O'Leary,
Four, five, six O'Leary,
Seven, eight, nine O'Leary,
Ten O'Learys sleeping.